Alex Timbers'

BROADWAY BIRD

· ILLUSTRATIONS BY ·

ALISA COBURN ·

Feiwel and Friends
New York

A FEIWEL AND FRIENDS BOOK
An imprint of Macmillan Publishing Group, LLC
120 Broadway, New York, NY 10271 • mackids.com

Our books may be purchased in bulk for promotional,
educational, or business use. Please contact your local
bookseller or the Macmillan Corporate and Premium Sales
Department at (800) 221-7945 ext. 5442 or by email at
MacmillanSpecialMarkets@macmillan.com.

Library of Congress Cataloging-in-Publication Data
is available.

First edition, 2022
Book design by Sharismar Rodriguez and Lisa Vega
Feiwel and Friends logo designed by Filomena Tuosto
Printed in China by RR Donnelley Asia Printing Solutions Ltd.,
Dongguan City, Guangdong Province

ISBN 978-1-250-78457-5 (hardcover)

10 9 8 7 6 5 4 3 2 1

To my wonderful mother and father,
who instilled in me a love of books,
birds, and Broadway —A. T.

For my gorgeous Nanna,
who loved budgies and glamour
in equal measure —A. C.

"Hello, my name is Louisa Parakeet, and I'm auditioning for the musical *Guys and Dogs.*"

She cleared her little parakeet throat
and then warbled beautifully.

Maybe the most beautiful rendition of
"If I Were a Beagle" that's ever been warbled.

The verdict came swift:

Sorry, 'keet. You're too small.

Who's going to pay big, big ticket prices to see such a teeny, tiny creature? Bye bye, birdie.

SIGN IN

WAIT HERE

But I can also

fly fast!

And I can

fly high!

"We're not looking for flying.
We're looking for singing and hoofing.
So come back when you got hoofs!"
The director burst into a horrendous
peal of outrageous snorts and laughter.

And Louisa was reminded
yet again what everyone knows:
You gotta be big to be on Broadway.

Louisa flew back home, past all the majestic theaters of Broadway.

What Louisa loved most about living in Times Square wasn't the *buzzzz* of the city or weaving between buildings or even all the free food on the cement sidewalks.

No, it was that she could sing as loud
as she wanted. She could sing all day and
she could sing all night.

Louisa was truly a Broadway bird.

Louisa arrived back home to her nest.

Rejected again?

Louisa hung her beak low.

"How am I ever going to get onstage, Sal?
I try and try, and I dream about it, but
all anyone sees is . . . this tiny bird."

For the opening night of *The Weasel of Oz*,
all the brightest stars of Broadway showed up, like
Patti LuPony, Cheetah Rivera, and Otter McDonald.

Louisa wouldn't miss a big Broadway opening.

Louisa snuck up to the rafters of the theater to watch.
She loved everything about *The Weasel of Oz*.

What she loved the most, though, was the climactic moment when
the great green actress Iguana Menzel, playing The Witch, was
hoisted on a rope high above the stage.

As Iguana sang out a spectacular final note, Louisa lamented hopelessly:

This is the part
I was hatched
to play . . .

Later that night, Louisa went to the famous Broadway watering hole, Sardine's. Her dream had never seemed so far away.

I've seen *that* expression before.

That, my friend, is the face of rejection.

Louisa shed a tiny tear.

"I just want to be on Broadway. I mean, I'm green, I can sing. I can even actually fly. They don't need a rope to make me soar high!"

She looked back at her food.
"But that's not how people see me,
I guess. I'm too tiny for that big stage."

The flamingo stared deeply at Louisa
for a moment, then sat down next to her.

"You know, years ago, before my long pink legs gave out, I was a dancer. I was the first bird on Broadway in the famous *Ziegfeld Water Fowl-lies of 1940.*

But before that,

I faced rejection

after rejection.

"Listen, 'keet, Broadway is about being big, with an exclamation point. But just because you're little doesn't mean you can't *be* big.

"You're only as small as you feel. And, birdy, do you *feel* small?"

Not at all!

Then go out there and show them how big you are!

The next morning, Louisa swooped into the audition room.

SEND
HER IN!

"I'm already here, ma'am,"
Louisa piped up. "Down below."

The director fumbled for her glasses and
squinted. "Oh yeah, you . . . *Polly Parakeet*.
Well, whatcha got for me today, Polly . . . ?"

Louisa proclaimed loudly and proudly,

My name is LOUISA PARAKEET and today I'll be singing 🎩 THE WITCH'S SONG ⭐ from my new favorite musical, *The WEASEL of Oz* ✦ ✦

The director could barely stifle her laughter.

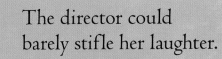

Um, okay. Sure. Go ahead.

And then Louisa went big.
Like, REALLY big.
Louisa danced all over the room.

She flew upside down
and danced on the ceiling.
She squawked. She tweeted!

She flew right up onto the director's table,
tap danced on it, and then soared high,
flapping her wings while singing
The Witch's climactic song.

TAP
TAPPITY
TAP!

There was nothing timid or
sweet about this parakeet.

When it was over, the director was silent.
She slowly removed her glasses.

"In all my years as a famous
canine director of the theater,
I've never seen a performer
like you."

"Tiny, yet powerful"

"Dramatic"

BROADWAY!

Louisa puffed up her feathers proudly.

"Listen, Polly, I have just the role for you. You'll be the understudy for the star of *The Weasel of Oz*. And then maybe someday, you rehearse and work hard enough, you'll play The Witch yourself."

She grabbed Louisa's wing with her scaly hand.

"Darling Louisa, there's room enough for two profoundly gifted green actresses on Broadway. Go out there now . . . and save our show!"

Louisa stood backstage, ready for her entrance.
She quietly mouthed along to every word,
sang along to every note, parroting them back.
This little songbird knew the show inside and out.

And then her cue came—

Louisa scampered out onstage and took off into the air,
belting out the climactic final song of the show.

She was *green,* she could *fly* . . .
and boy, could she *sing*!

And there wasn't a single person in that audience
who couldn't see little Louisa Parakeet.

The crowd exploded with cheers!
Louisa looked out at them and realized in that moment . . .

she had just performed on Broadway.

Hours later, Louisa signed autograph after autograph outside the stage door.

Everyone wanted to know who Louisa was, where she had trained, and *could they have a photo with this extraordinarily talented parakeet?* Louisa was happy to oblige each and every one of them.

Finally, a determined but shy young elephant pushed through the crowd. "Ms. Parakeet, I want to be a Broadway star like you. But people say I'm too big to be on Broadway. Do you have any advice?"

Louisa looked up at him after finishing signing the sweet pachyderm's playbill, and she smiled.

You're perfect as you are.

And with talent and hard work, you can be anything.

MEET THE BROADWAY STARS! CAN YOU FIND THEM IN THIS BOOK?

LEN CARIBOU

Cariou is a Canadian actor and director who is best known for playing the lead role in the original production of *Sweeney Todd*.

BILLY GOAT PORTER

Winner of a Tony Award for his performance onstage in *Kinky Boots*, Porter is also a successful recording artist, director, and an influential LGBTQ icon.

LEMUR SALONGA

Salonga is a beloved singer and actress who originated the lead role in the musical *Miss Saigon*. She is also the first Asian woman to win a Tony award!

EARTHA KITTEN

Famous for everything from her singing and dancing to her comedy and activism, Kitt was an Emmy and Tony award–nominated star.

ANGELA LAMBSBURY

Lansbury's career spans eight decades and many, many award nominations. On Broadway, she starred in shows like *Gypsy*, *Sweeney Todd*, and *The King and I*.

PATTI LUPONY

Over five decades, LuPone (a native New Yorker) has starred in many successful Broadway musicals such as *Anything Goes*, *Evita*, *Sweeney Todd*, and *Company*.

OTTER McDONALD

McDonald made her Broadway debut in *The Secret Garden* and, since that time, has gone on to an illustrious stage career, winning six Tony Awards.

IGUANA MENZEL

Known for her incredible vocal belt, Menzel was an original cast member of popular Broadway musicals *Rent* and *Wicked.*

JESSIE MULE-ER

Mueller began her career in Chicago, where she quickly gained acclaim and went on to star in the musicals *Waitress* and *Beautiful: The Carole King Musical* in New York.

KELLI O'HARE

Known for her glittering soprano, O'Hara is a Tony-winning star who works equally on Broadway, television, and at the Metropolitan Opera.

JOEL GREYHOUND

Grey is a multitalented actor, singer, dancer, director, and photographer known for his roles in *Cabaret*, *Chicago*, and the original Broadway cast of *Wicked.*

CHEETAH RIVERA

Rivera originated the roles of Anita in *West Side Story* and Velma in *Chicago*, and she appeared in the movie adaptation of *Sweet Charity.*

GENE PELLY

An iconic actor and filmmaker who revitalized the Hollywood musical, Kelly got his start as a Broadway dancer in the 1938 Cole Porter musical *Leave It to Me!*

ELAINE OSTRICH

Brassy and acerbic, Stritch made her Broadway debut in 1946 and went on to receive four Tony nominations, notably for the Stephen Sondheim musical *Company.*

DICK VAN DUCK

Best known for his sitcom *The Dick Van Dyke Show* and his iconic appearance in the movie *Mary Poppins*, Van Dyke is also a Tony-winning Broadway actor.

AUTHOR'S NOTE

One thing I've always been struck by as a native New Yorker is the way that birds are such an integral part of New York City's fabric. We see them every day. We live alongside them. They're as New York as skyscrapers or taxicabs.

When I was young, my mother and I raised budgies and finches. I adored them. I know they're not as glamorous as dogs or cats and that people don't make movies or write epic novels about tiny parakeets. But they're fascinating, funny little songbirds, and there's a reason they are so popular.

As a stage director, I've often thought about why I'm so drawn to making theater in the first place. For me, it's a passion that ignited in high school. It was never about success, money, or the fabulously elaborate costumes and scenery. It was about a sense of community, a shared passion among a group of outsiders; it was about *finding one's own flock.*

And so, when I began thinking about how to tell a story about that same passion and sense of belonging in the Broadway theater scene, I thought back to those unsung heroes of New York City life: the birds that inhabit my city.

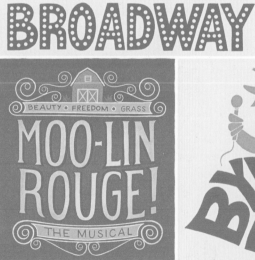